Watch

JOYCE SHAPPEE

ILLUSTRATED BY ANNETTE WOOD

Illustration by Annette Wood: www.AnnetteWoodGraphics.com

ISBN: 979-8-99-16319-0-7

Printed in the United States

To all the backyard birds
that have entertained and
given me wonderment throughout my life.
May you do the same for all
who read this book.

J. D. Shappee
September 2024

Watch

The Red-Winged Blackbird
Float in the sky.

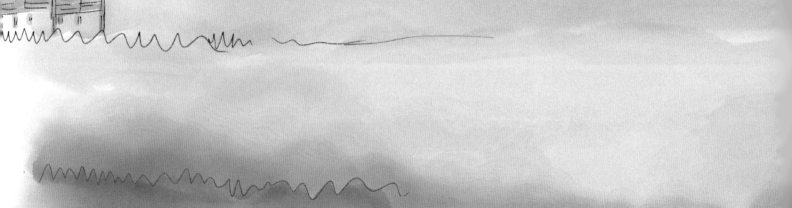

Watch

The Blue Jay
Soar by.

Watch

The Phoebe
Dressed in his tuxedo
Flit from space to Space.
As he guards his territory
With rapid pace.

Watch

The Hummingbird
Sitting so erect on the branch.
Offering a warning chatter,
As he, too, protects his space.

Watch

The Barn Swallows
Like rockets in the sky.
Dart in and out catching insects,
So their fledglings can survive.

Watch

Doves balance on wires
Basking in the sun.
Cooing to each other
That another day has begun.

Watch

The Red-Tailed Hawk fly high.
Calling to its young nested fledgling
Challenging it to take a leap
It's first flight soaring into the deep.

Watch

House Finches, Sparrows, and Warblers alike
Gracefully gliding the morning azure sky.
Freely giving callings of love songs
To all that, Watch.

About the Backyard Birds

Red-Winged Black Bird

These birds are found all over the United States. Red-Winged Black Birds feed on fruits, grains and sometimes insects. In the spring males ruffle out their red wings to attract females and defend their territory from other males.

Blue Jay

Depending on where you live in the United States, there are different kinds of Blue Jay's. California has two species, the Steller's Jay and the Western Scrub Jay. The Steller's Jay feathers are blue, and its head is black crested. The Western Scrub Jay has no crest and has blue and white feathers accented in gray. They both forage the ground looking for insects, nuts and seeds to eat.

Black Phoebe

Phoebes are part of the Flycatcher species. They are usually seen singly and are territorial. They eat insects and small fruit. Phoebe's capture the insect in mid-air. Their mud nests are built under bridges or eaves. Females and males look very similar making it hard to distinguish them from each other.

Hummingbird

Hummingbirds are the smallest bird in the world. They drink nectar from flowers and will on occasion eat an insect either stolen mid-flight or from a spider web. The hummingbird also uses the web of the spider to make its nest.

Barn Swallow

Barn Swallows only eat insects taken in the air. Its tail is forked helping it soar and giving it better mobility. Barn Swallows nest in groups sharing food with each other's fledglings. The nests are made of mud and built under bridges and eaves.

Morning Dove

Doves are found all over the United States. They eat grains, seeds and fruit found mainly on the ground. Nests are simply made from twigs, or plant fibers. Doves join together for life. The male brings the twigs to the female, and she makes the nest.

Red-Tailed Hawk

In general, female Red-Tailed Hawks are larger than the males. Red-Tailed Hawks eat a wide variety of mammals, including other birds, reptiles and rodents.

Both the male and female help build the nests and often reuse the nests. The Red-Tailed Hawk is often seen along roadsides perching on telephone wires searching for their next meal.

House Finches, Sparrows, and Warblers

These are all backyard birds who forage bird feeders and take drinks and baths at outdoor fountains. They mainly eat nuts, grains, and small fruit. They also feed from the ground or low vegetation. They live in a variety of places from deserts to suburban backyards. Their nests are usually built in trees made from twigs and compost.